The Midnight Mystery

Beverly Lewis

Beverly Lewis Books for Young Readers

Picture Books

Cows in the House
Annika's Secret Wish

The Cul-de-sac Kids

The Double Dabble Surprise
The Chicken Pox Panic
The Crazy Christmas Angel Mystery
No Grown-ups Allowed
Frog Power
The Mystery of Case D. Luc
The Stinky Sneakers Mystery
Pickle Pizza
Mailbox Mania
The Mudhole Mystery
Fiddlesticks
The Crabby Cat Caper
Tarantula Toes
Green Gravy
Backyard Bandit Mystery
Tree House Trouble
The Creepy Sleep-Over
The Great TV Turn-Off
Piggy Party
The Granny Game
Mystery Mutt
Big Bad Beans
The Upside-Down Day
The Midnight Mystery

Katie and Jake and the Haircut Mistake

01A

The Midnight Mystery

Beverly Lewis

BETHANY HOUSE PUBLISHERS
MINNEAPOLIS, MINNESOTA 55438

The Midnight Mystery

Cover illustration by Paul Turnbaugh
Cover design by the Lookout Design Group, Inc.
Text illustrations by Janet Huntington

Published by Bethany House Publishers
A Ministry of Bethany Fellowship International
11400 Hampshire Avenue South
Bloomington, Minnesota 55438
www.bethanyhouse.com

Printed in the United States of America by
Bethany Press International, Bloomington, Minnesota 55438

Library of Congress Cataloging-in-Publication Data

Lewis, Beverly, 1949–
The midnight mystery / by Beverly Lewis.
p. cm. — (The cul-de-sac kids ; 24)
Summary: After an ice cream party to celebrate the last day of school, Dunkum's cousin Ellen's seeing-eye-dog disappears, and the Cul-de-sac Kids get help from an unexpected source in solving the mystery.
ISBN 0–7642–2129–9 (pbk.)
[1. Guide dogs—Fiction. 2. Dogs—Fiction. 3. Clubs—Fiction. 4. Mystery and detective stories.] I. Title.
PZ7.L58464 Mi 2001
[Fic]—dc21

00-011572

For
Kahla Erickson,
who loves to read.
And
for Erin Meyer,
who loves to write.

THE CUL-DE-SAC KIDS

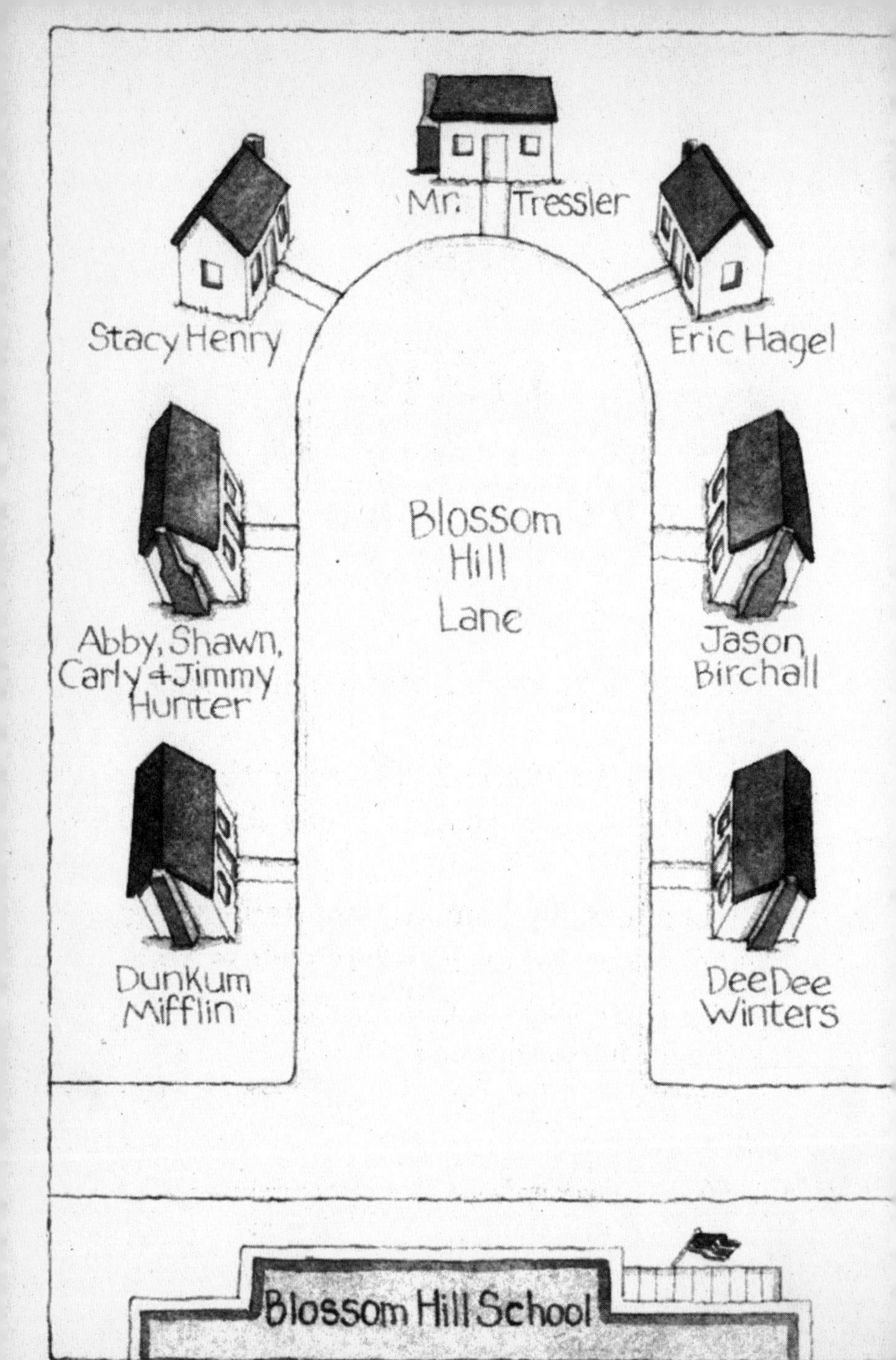
Mr. Tressler
Stacy Henry
Eric Hagel
Blossom
Hill
Lane
Abby, Shawn,
Carly & Jimmy
Hunter
Jason
Birchall
Dunkum
Mifflin
Dee Dee
Winters
Blossom Hill School

ONE

The end of the school year had come. At last!

Dunkum Mifflin had been counting the days. He was rip-roaring ready for summer.

He and Abby Hunter stood tall on the school stage. Miss Hershey's class was taking their curtain call. They bowed low as the audience clapped.

Yahoo! End of school, thought Dunkum.

The audience kept clapping.

Then . . . *swoosh!* The stage curtains dropped and the lights went up. The Blossom Hill School spring play was finished. A smashing success.

Dunkum and Abby hurried backstage. The other Cul-de-sac Kids were waiting in the wings, behind the curtains. They were all smiles.

Abby was the president of the block club. Five boys and four girls. They loved adventure and solving mysteries. Their club slogan was "Cul-de-sac Kids stick together."

Dunkum removed his space-captain suit. Carefully, he placed it in the props box. "What a cool play," he said.

Abby's eyes danced. "Lots better than last year!"

"Yep, sure was," Jason Birchall said. He was prancing and jiving about, as usual.

Eric Hagel and Jason gave Dunkum

and Abby high fives. "All the practicing paid off," said Eric.

"Time to celebrate!" said Jason.

"Everyone's coming to my house," Dunkum said, grinning. He had sent out invitations for an ice-cream party.

Jason's eyes grew bigger. "What are we waiting for?" he asked. "Let's get going."

Eric and Stacy Henry agreed. "Junk food, here we come," Stacy said. And Eric gave a thumbs-up.

"We won't be in Miss Hershey's class *next* year," Jason said. He tossed his space costume into the props box.

"Don't worry about that now," Dunkum said. "Summer's finally here!"

Dunkum's blind cousin, Ellen Mifflin, came around the curtains. Honey, her guide dog, led the way. The dog wore a shiny blue space suit and black wire antennas. He had played a poochy part in the play—Space Dog.

Abby and her younger sister, Carly, and Carly's best friend, Dee Dee Winters, crowded around Space Dog. "So . . . how does Honey like show business?" asked Abby.

Ellen's eyes were closed. "Oh, she loves it. Don't you, girl?" She knelt down and hugged her dog. Ellen's long brown hair covered Honey's face.

"Wait till you see her brand-new tricks," Dunkum said. He took off the dog's costume and antennas.

"You're kidding. New tricks?" Abby asked. She sat beside Stacy, near Honey. The boys crowded around, too.

Ellen stood up, smiling. "Honey loves to perform. Don't you, big girl?"

"Woof, woof!" barked Honey.

"Give us a sneak preview," Eric pleaded.

A mischievous grin swept across Ellen's face. "Wait for the party," she said.

"Aw, why not now?" Jason begged.

"Because I need ice cream for the trick," Ellen said. She pushed her hair behind her ear.

"That reminds me," Dunkum said, looking at Jason. "Are you hungry for chocolate ice cream?"

Jason licked his lips and rubbed his stomach. "Wild pit bulls couldn't keep me away."

"Don't you mean wild *horses*?" Dunkum said.

"Horses . . . pit bulls, whatever." Jason pranced around.

"I know a good pit bull joke," Ellen said. She held on to her dog's harness. "Want to hear it?"

Honey barked and shook her head.

"Hey, it looks like Honey just said no." Jason and the Cul-de-sac Kids watched Ellen's guide dog closely.

"Better cover Honey's ears when you

talk about pit bulls," Dunkum joked.

Ellen giggled, feeling for Honey's ears. "There," she said, finding them. "Now, what did the pit bull say when he sat on a pile of sandpaper?"

The kids looked at one another. They shrugged their shoulders.

"I think we give up," Dunkum said, eager to know. "What *did* the pit bull say when he sat on the sandpaper?"

Ellen's eyes were open, but they stared straight ahead. " 'Rough, rough,' " she giggled.

"Hey, that's a good joke," Jason said as he headed for the door. He was usually the last person to arrive anywhere. But when it came to sweets, Jason Birchall was first in line!

Dunkum's parents waved from the back of the room. "We'll see you at the party," Dunkum's dad called.

Dunkum's house was across the street

from the school. He and his friends were going to walk to the party.

Abby and Stacy followed Ellen and her guide dog down the stage steps. Jason and Eric joined the girls near the outside door. So did Dunkum.

Adam Henny, a kid with dirt on his face, showed up just then. "Where's everyone going?" he asked.

"No place special," Dunkum lied.

Adam was the last person Dunkum wanted hanging around. Adam's clothes looked like toxic waste dump specials. Especially the ratty red T-shirt he had on.

Besides that, Adam Henny was *not* a Cul-de-sac Kid. No way was Dunkum going to invite an outsider to his party!

TWO

Dunkum couldn't wait to leave. "Have a nice summer," he said to Adam.

The dirty kid smiled a faint smile. He pushed his hand into his pants pocket and pulled out something. "Here's my phone number."

Dunkum shook his head. "Uh, no, that's OK," he said and rushed out the door. He wanted to forget about Adam. No sense messing up the end-of-school party over *that* kid.

The Cul-de-sac Kids were waiting at

the flagpole. "What kind of ice-cream toppings are we having?" asked Jason.

"That's not polite," Eric piped up. "Just wait and see."

Dunkum elbowed Eric's ribs. "Hey, relax, Eric. School's out. It's pig-out time!" He began to name off all the toppings. "Jelly beans, chocolate sprinkles, strawberry syrup . . ." He paused. "Uh, I forgot the rest."

"Come on, try!" Jason pleaded.

"Dunkum's always forgetting stuff," Ellen said.

"It's a good thing Abby's our club president," Dunkum said. "*She* never forgets anything."

"And don't you forget it," Abby agreed.

It was true. Dunkum was a good detective only because Abby and the others were his partners. She paid attention to details. So far they'd solved every mystery known to man. Well . . . at least the ones on Blossom Hill Lane.

Dunkum waited at the curb for Honey to step into the street. Ellen gripped the harness with her left hand. "Honey, forward," she said.

But Honey waited for two more cars. When it was safe, she led Ellen across. "Good girl," Ellen said.

A black jeep was parked in the driveway across the street. On the back was a bumper sticker. It read *I ♥ pets!* A bald man was holding a fluffy, gray cat.

"Hey, that's Mister Whiskers!" Dee Dee said, racing across the street.

"What's that man doing with your cat?" Dunkum asked, staring.

The man turned and frowned. "Poor thing. I found him just wandering around," he explained. He gave Dee Dee her cat.

"That's strange," Abby said. "I thought he stayed in the house."

"Mister Whiskers?" The man looked at the cat in Dee Dee's arms. "What a nice name." He stroked the kitten, but his eyes seemed very dark. At least Dunkum thought so.

"Mister Whiskers is a cool Cul-de-sac Cat," Jason said, nodding his head.

The man turned and looked at Honey. "That's one nice dog you've got there," he said.

"Thanks," Ellen said. "She's my eyes."

"I can see that," the man said. Suddenly, he got into his car.

"Thanks for taking care of my cat," Dee Dee called to him.

"Anytime," the man said out his car window.

The kids raced to Dunkum's house.

Party time!

★ ★ ★

In the kitchen, a row of ice-cream toppings lined the table.

Jason was the first to be served. "Hey, look!" he said. "There's a worm in my ice cream." He held up something green and wiggly. He waved it at Carly Hunter.

"Ee-ew!" squealed Carly as Jason dropped the green Gummi Worm into his mouth.

Dunkum and Eric ate two worms each. Just plain.

Abby, Stacy, and Carly asked for waffle cones. Dunkum's father scooped up chocolate ice cream for them. He pushed the ice cream into their cones. "Some worms for the ladies?" he asked, smiling.

"Not for me, thanks," Stacy replied.

"How about sprinkles?" Dunkum's dad asked.

The girls nodded. "Sprinkles are fine, thanks," Abby said.

"They're really chocolate-covered ants,

you know. Fried and dried," Dunkum teased.

"Double dabble yuck," Abby said, giggling. She slid in beside Ellen at the table.

Honey lay close to Ellen's feet, taking a snooze. The dog seemed at home in Dunkum's house. Ellen did, too.

Ellen's dad was out of the country with an overseas job. Dunkum didn't mind at all. It was lots of fun having Ellen and Honey visit.

Dunkum's mom dished up some ice cream for Ellen. Honey's nose twitched, and she opened one eye. "I think it's time for Honey's performance," Dunkum said.

Eric sat across the table. He wiped off his chocolate mustache with a napkin. "Go for it."

Ellen reached down and touched her dog's head. "Honey, let's play Lickety-split."

Dunkum made a drum-roll on the table.

All the kids watched closely.

Honey stood up. The tips of her ears stood at attention. She kept her eyes on Ellen. Only Ellen.

"Hey, check it out. The dog obeys better than I do," Jason said, laughing.

"Honey is real smart," Dunkum said. "Just watch."

THREE

Dunkum scooped up some ice cream. He put it in a cone for Ellen. "One vanilla cone coming up," he said.

"Woof, woof!" Honey barked.

Ellen smiled. "You like this trick, don't you, girl?"

Honey barked again.

Dunkum handed the cone to Ellen. She held it in front of her and gave the command. "Honey, take two licks. But only two."

Honey's tongue slurped the cone. Twice.

All the kids clapped.

"That's double dabble amazing!" Abby said. "Our dog would *never* do that."

"Nope," little Carly said. "Our dog would bite the cone right out of your hand!"

"Wait . . . there's more," Ellen said softly.

Honey waited. Ears perked, tongue out.

Ellen gave the command. "Honey, take three licks."

The kids counted, "1 . . . 2 . . . 3," as Honey licked the cone.

Eric slapped his forehead. "I don't believe this!"

"I not, either," said Shawn, Abby's Korean brother.

"Tell Honey to take twenty licks," Jason shouted.

"She doesn't know that number," Ellen

said. "But she knows *this*." Ellen held up the cone again.

Honey looked up at the ice cream.

"Honey," Ellen whispered. "Lickety-split!"

Carefully, Honey opened her mouth wide and held the cone in it. She carried the cone across the room without eating it.

Then she stood on her hind legs and tossed the cone up . . . up into the air.

Poof!

In one gulp, the ice cream—cone and all—disappeared into the dog's mouth.

The kids shouted with delight, "Do it again!"

Honey licked her chops and gave Ellen a kiss. Dunkum quickly made another cone.

And Honey did the trick again.

Soon, it was time for the Cul-de-sac Kids to go home. Dunkum followed his friends to the door.

"Thanks for the party," Carly said. She waved while her second ice-cream cone dripped off her hand. Vanilla drops dripped all the way down the sidewalk.

"Your party was fun, Dunkum," said Stacy. "Even the fried ants." She made a face and giggled with Abby.

"See you tomorrow." Dunkum waved to them.

That's when he saw something red flash in the bushes across the street!

White moonbeams cast their shadows on Blossom Hill Lane. Dunkum stared at the bushes.

Was someone in a red shirt hiding over there? Or were his eyes playing a trick on him?

FOUR

Dunkum rubbed his eyes, still watching.

I saw something, he thought. *I just know it!*

"It's bedtime," called his mother from the house.

Dunkum didn't go back inside. Instead, he ran across the street. He searched the bushes and found some old newspapers.

Then he saw an ID bracelet. Dunkum picked it up. The letters A. H. shone in the moonlight.

A.H.

A. H.? Must belong to Abby Hunter, he thought.

Dunkum looked up the street. He could see Abby, Carly, and their adopted brothers walking with Stacy.

He shook his head. "There's no way Abby could've dropped this. Not way over here."

He stuffed the bracelet into his pocket and headed back across the street. Looking down, he saw vanilla ice-cream globs on the sidewalk. "What a mess," he whispered.

He remembered seeing Carly's ice-cream cone drip on the sidewalk as she left. He hurried inside to get some wet paper towels. He wanted to clean up the mess before his mother found it. And before any ants started showing up. "Mom hates ants," he muttered.

He left the front door open and dashed into the kitchen.

Ellen was still sitting at the table, humming softly. "I'm too tired to put Honey's harness back on," she said with a yawn.

Dunkum glanced at Honey. "Looks like she's zonked out," he said. "Here, I'll help you upstairs."

His mother was cleaning up the kitchen.

"Okay if Honey sleeps here tonight, Mom?" Dunkum asked.

She looked at the sleeping dog under the table. "Honey looks comfortable right there."

Ellen stood up. "Sweet dreams, girl," she whispered to Honey. Then she blew a kiss.

Dunkum bent his right elbow and guided Ellen upstairs. "The party was fun," he said.

"I don't think Honey had enough ice cream," Ellen said. "She would have done that Lickey-split trick at least two more times."

"Too much sugar might rot her teeth," Dunkum said. "Unless she brushes right away."

Ellen laughed.

"Well, good night," Dunkum said and headed to the kitchen.

Honey was still asleep under the table. Dunkum watched the steady rise and fall of her breathing. "Sleep tight, Honey," he said.

He hugged his parents good-night and went to his room. Putting on his pajamas, Dunkum thought of Adam Henny. Dirty, rotten Adam probably didn't own a single pair of pj's. And he had hardly one good friend.

Dunkum skipped saying his prayers tonight. He hopped into bed and snuggled down. Strings of moonbeams danced on the pillow as he fell asleep.

At midnight, Dunkum sat straight up in bed.

Something had popped into his memory. Something so important it woke him up!

"Oh," he groaned. "How could I forget?"

Grabbing his bathrobe, he darted through the hall and down the stairs. He flicked on the inside switch, flooding the front yard with light. Dunkum opened the front door and looked at the sidewalk.

Phooey!

The ants had already come. They were having an ice-cream party parade!

Dunkum tiptoed to the kitchen and yanked on the towel rack. The roll went flying. He crawled under the table and chased the roll of paper towels.

Right away, he noticed the empty spot under the table. Right where Honey had been sleeping.

"Honey?" he called softly, looking around the kitchen.

Dunkum placed the paper towel roll on the rack and rushed upstairs. He opened Ellen's door without making a sound. Peering into Ellen's room, he said, "Are you in there, Honey?"

Ellen made a squeaky little sound in her sleep.

He didn't want to awaken and worry her. So he closed the bedroom door and flew back downstairs.

He looked everywhere for Honey. In the living room, under the coffee table. He looked in the dining room, under the dinner table. He even looked in the garage.

"What's happened to Ellen's dog?" Dunkum whispered. He felt sick inside.

Honey was missing!

He sat on a kitchen chair and stared at the floor where Honey had slept. Where *was* she?

Ellen would need Honey first thing tomorrow. And Ellen's father was coming for her next week!

Dunkum had to find Honey.

Soon!

FIVE

Dunkum's heart pounded.

He grabbed a flashlight and headed to the dimly lit basement. Slowly, he shone his flashlight into the darkest corners. Light zigzagged across boxes of Christmas ornaments.

Flash! He shined the light on rows of canned goods. But Honey was nowhere in sight.

Dashing upstairs, Dunkum ran outside, past the party ants. He spotted something lying in the grass. At first it looked like a fake red snake. He leaned down. "What's this?" he said softly.

It was a leather collar. Just like Honey's collar. Dunkum read the tags. It *was* Honey's collar!

His eyes caught the swarm of ants. He'd forgotten again! But instead of going inside for paper towels, he marched to the outside faucet. He would hose down the ice-cream drippings, ants and all!

Just as Dunkum turned on the hose, a light flashed on above his head. He looked up to see his parents' bedroom, filled with light.

Oh, rats, he thought.

Turning off the hose, he ran toward the house.

But his father met him at the door. "What's going on, son? Why are you outside at midnight?"

Dunkum opened his mouth to speak.

"Don't you know what time it is?" His

father tapped on his watch.

"It's late," Dunkum blurted, trying to explain. "I think Honey left the house." He held up her collar.

"You *think*?"

Dunkum's mother was coming down the stairs. He stood in the doorway, hoping to block her view of the ants.

Dad told Mom the bad news. "Dunkum says Honey's missing, dear."

"What?" Mom let out a little wail. "Are you sure? Have you searched the house and the yard?"

Dunkum nodded. "I've looked everywhere."

"Who was the last person to see Honey?" Dad asked.

Dunkum wasn't sure. "I think Ellen was the last person to see Honey." It sounded dumb because Ellen couldn't see at all.

"You know, I had a real strange feeling

about Honey sleeping downstairs tonight." Dunkum's mom pushed the front door shut. "By the way, this door was standing wide open when I went to bed."

"It was?" Dunkum had forgotten that, too.

"Well, that's it, then," his father said. "Honey took off sometime after Ellen went to bed."

Dunkum felt horrible. Guide dogs were special. Lots of time went into training them. Lots of money, too. Besides that, Honey was part of the family.

A lump the size of a scoop of ice cream filled his throat.

Dunkum's mother pushed her bangs back. "Honey will probably come home when she's hungry."

"Hungry? That's it!" Dunkum shouted.

His parents watched in amazement as Dunkum led them out the front door. "I think I just remembered!" He pointed to the sidewalk.

His mom gasped. "Oh, look at those horrid ants!"

Dunkum tried to explain. "After the party, Carly's cone was dripping onto the sidewalk."

Suddenly, Dad seemed to understand. "And we all know how much Honey loves vanilla ice cream," he said. The lines in his forehead grew deeper.

"Honey must've followed the drips," Dunkum's mom said.

"So . . . she might be somewhere up the street," Dunkum said. "Maybe even at Abby's house." He started up the sidewalk.

"It's midnight," his mom called to him. "It's much too late to search now."

"That's right," Dad said. "Honey will be all right until morning."

But Dunkum was worried. Honey was trained to guide blind Ellen. Who knows what dangers were lurking in the midnight shadows?

Tears stung Dunkum's eyes. This was all his fault.

SIX

The next morning, Dunkum hurried downstairs.

Was Mom right? Had Honey come home for breakfast?

He searched the front yard, then the back. Honey was nowhere to be seen.

He ran through the neighborhood and asked each Cul-de-sac Kid if they'd seen Honey.

Nobody had.

"Let's trace the ice-cream trail," Abby suggested when she heard the whole story.

The kids agreed.

So, starting at Dunkum's house, they counted twenty ice-cream drops to Abby's house.

"Look, you can even see Honey's tongue marks," said Jason.

Eric looked closer. "Cannot."

"Gotcha!" hooted Jason.

Abby frowned, ignoring Jason. "What other clues do we have?" she asked Dunkum.

He showed Honey's dog collar and the ID bracelet. "This is all I found last night . . . at midnight."

Eric looked at the bracelet. He studied the initials. "A. H.? Maybe it belongs to Abby."

"It's not mine." Abby twisted her hair. "Think of all the kids we know with those initials."

"I'll make a list of people's names," Stacy offered.

"Good idea," Eric said.

The kids split up and hopped on their bikes. Up and down the street they rode, whistling and calling for Honey. They talked to each neighbor on Blossom Hill Lane. They even checked at the Humane Society, where lost pets are kept.

But no Honey.

At last they followed Dunkum into his house. Ellen was having breakfast. Her eyes were red from crying.

Dunkum raced into the kitchen. "We're going to find Honey for you," he said. "I promise."

"We'll do our detective best," Abby said and gave Ellen a hug.

"Let's put an ad in the paper," Dunkum said. "If someone sees Honey, we might get a phone call."

Abby suggested, "We could offer a reward."

"Hey, good thinking. That ought to

help," Jason said. He held up the newspaper. "Look, here's someone offering twenty dollars for a brown beagle." The kids crowded around Jason.

Stacy pulled out a pencil and a pad. "If we each give some of our allowance, we'll have enough for a nice reward," she said.

"Don't count Ellen," Eric said. "It wouldn't be fair for her to put money into a reward."

"I think twenty bucks is too cheap," Dunkum said. "Let's go with closer to forty."

So the reward for finding and returning Honey would be thirty-six dollars.

Dunkum divided nine kids into thirty-six bucks, leaving Ellen out. "Four dollars each," he told them.

"Not bad," said Dee Dee.

"I have more than that in my piggy bank," said Carly.

"Me too," said little Jimmy Hunter.

"It'll be worth it to have Honey back," Abby said. "Now, let's decide on our ad."

★ ★ ★

LOST—
one golden Labrador guide dog.
Answers to Honey.
$36 reward.
Call 555-1028
or return to
233 Blossom Hill Lane.

"I really hope this works," Ellen said. She wiped her eyes.

"We *all* do," said Dunkum.

SEVEN

"Let's ride our bikes to the newspaper office," Dunkum said.

The Cul-de-sac Kids called their good-byes to Ellen.

On the way, they saw a dogcatcher. Dunkum cringed. Honey had lost her collar last night. What if the pound found her? How would a beautiful, smart dog like Honey feel locked up with mangy mutts?

"Hey, mister!" Dunkum called. "Have you seen a golden Lab around the neighborhood?"

The Cul-de-sac Kids stopped pedaling.

Jimmy Hunter's eyes were wide as saucers. His older brother, Shawn, looked very worried. Carly and Dee Dee whispered to each other. Abby and Stacy were silent. Eric pulled his bike up next to Jason's.

The dogcatcher walked toward them, mopping his forehead. "Sorry, kids. No dogs like that around here."

"Thanks anyway," Dunkum said. He felt kind of sad. But glad, too, that Honey wasn't considered a stray.

The kids pushed on, past the corner store. When they came to the post office, Dunkum spotted Adam Henny. He was mailing a letter, wearing one of his Ratty R Us outfits.

Dunkum sped up. He hoped Adam wouldn't see him. Because Adam Henny was the last person Dunkum wanted to talk to today.

"Yo, Dunkum! Wait up!" It was Adam shouting at him.

The Cul-de-sac Kids slowed down. Abby waved to Adam. So did Eric and Jason. Jimmy and Shawn rode their bikes over to Adam.

Dunkum gripped his handlebars, watching his friends. He felt too tense. He did *not* want shabby Adam in their club!

"Where's everyone going?" Adam asked Abby.

Dunkum took a deep breath. He wanted to say, "Get lost."

But Abby said, "Ellen's dog is missing. We're putting an ad in the newspaper."

Adam looked surprised. "Honey's missing?"

"Uh, we better get going," Dunkum interrupted. He wanted to get away from Adam. Fast.

So he led the group, speeding off and leaving the dirty boy behind. Once again.

"Dunkum, wait!" Adam called after them. But Dunkum would not look back.

★ ★ ★

At the newspaper office, Abby shoved her kickstand down. She glared at Dunkum. "What's your problem?" she asked. "You were rude to Adam. Why?"

"I don't want him in on our plans," Dunkum shouted back at her.

"What's the big deal? Nobody said it was a secret about Honey," Abby said. Her hands were on her hips. She seemed angry.

Eric stepped between them. "Don't yell at her, Dunkum. Abby didn't do anything wrong."

"Yeah, who cares if Adam knows?" Jason asked.

Dunkum was no dummy. Eric and Jason were sticking up for Abby. "Adam Henny isn't a Cul-de-sac Kid. That's all,"

Dunkum muttered. "He's not in our club."

"Well, so what?" Stacy spoke up. "He's a human being, isn't he?"

The kids stared at her, surprised. Stacy hardly ever raised her voice.

"It doesn't matter if Adam is in our club or not," Abby shot back. "He can help us find Honey, can't he?"

Dunkum was afraid Abby might say that. No way should Adam get the reward money.

Eric shrugged his shoulders. "Adam's not so bad." He turned and followed Abby up the steps to the newspaper office.

The Cul-de-sac Kids were close behind.

Dunkum stomped his foot. His summer was off to a rotten start. Thanks to a kid who needed a two-hour bath!

EIGHT

When Dunkum arrived home, Ellen was reading her Braille joke book. "Listen to this," she said.

Dunkum sat down. He was glad Ellen couldn't see his face. He was also glad she couldn't see into his heart.

"Who was the world's first banker?" she asked.

"I don't know," said Dunkum, trying to sound interested.

"Pharaoh's daughter. She found a little prophet in the rushes to the banks." Ellen began to laugh. "Isn't that funny?"

"Yeah, real funny," Dunkum said, pouting.

"What's wrong with you?" Ellen asked, facing him.

"How can you read jokes and laugh when Honey's missing?"

"God will take care of Honey," she said.

Dunkum felt terrible. He was getting it from all sides. Excusing himself, he went to his room. Every few minutes, he could hear Ellen laughing out loud.

The joke book must be very funny, thought Dunkum.

He decided to sit in his room, all by himself.

★ ★ ★

An hour later, the doorbell rang. "I'll get it," Dunkum said. He rushed downstairs.

Eric Hagel stood on the porch.

"Hi, Eric. What's up?" Dunkum asked.

"Let's talk somewhere private," Eric said. His eyes blinked too fast.

"Come to my room," Dunkum said, leading the way.

"Where's that ID bracelet you showed us?" Eric asked.

Dunkum went to his dresser and picked up the bracelet. "What do you want with it?"

"I think I know who it belongs to," Eric said. He took it from Dunkum. "I think A. H. stands for Adam Henny."

Dunkum gasped. "Of course!" Why hadn't he thought of that?

"But . . . we don't know for sure," Eric added.

"It makes sense, though, doesn't it?" Dunkum said.

"Only if Adam dropped it in the bushes last night," Eric said.

"Adam must've been spying on our

party," Dunkum decided.

"That's strange." Eric sat on Dunkum's bed. "Do you think this is a dognapping case?" he asked.

"Beats me," Dunkum said. "Let's have a club meeting. We'll see what the rest of the Cul-de-sac Kids think."

"Ellen should come, too," Eric said.

"You're right. She has sort of a sixth sense," Dunkum said.

They hurried downstairs to get Ellen.

★ ★ ★

The club meeting was in Abby's backyard. She called the meeting to order. Then she said, "Any new business?"

Dunkum held up the ID bracelet. "Eric and I have a theory. We think this clue might lead us to Honey."

Abby and Stacy sat in the grass, twirling their hair.

Carly and Dee Dee were all ears.

"What's a theory?" asked Dee Dee.

"It's like a guess," Dunkum explained.

"I don't want to guess about Honey," Jimmy said.

Shawn shook his head. He was worried about Honey, too.

Eric was grinning. "Dunkum and I guess that this ID bracelet belongs to Adam Henny."

Abby's mouth flew open. "Why do you think that?"

"For one thing, there are only two kids with A. H. initials," Dunkum said. He glanced at Abby.

Ellen asked to hold the ID bracelet. She had a strange look on her face as she touched it.

"If this *does* belong to Adam," Dunkum said, "I think we're looking at a dognapping."

"Wha-at?" Abby and Ellen said together.

"It could be a case for the police," Dunkum said. Talking about the police made him feel much better.

If Adam Henny was to blame, maybe *then* he'd leave them alone.

NINE

The next day, Dunkum talked to Abby after Sunday school. "I'm sorry about yesterday," he said.

"You were upset. So was I." She paused for a moment. "You know what?"

"What?" asked Dunkum.

"I'm sorry, too," she said.

Dunkum waited in line at the water fountain. "Did you see our ad in the morning paper?" he asked.

Abby smiled, her eyes shining. "It looked terrific. But something's strange.

There were sixteen pets reported missing over the weekend."

"Wow, that's a lot," Dunkum said.

"I think something's going on," she said.

"What do you mean?" Dunkum asked.

"I did some checking," Abby told him. "I called six of the people who placed ads for lost pets."

"You did?" Dunkum was all ears. "What did they say?"

"It seems that a bald man in a black jeep has been returning lost pets," said Abby. "And, get this. Each owner had offered a reward."

Dunkum whistled. "Sounds like some nice guy."

"Unless he's stealing them first and giving them back for money," Abby said.

"Hey, what a rotten thing to do!" Dunkum said.

"If we could just find that man, maybe

we'd find Honey," Abby said.

Dunkum was silent, thinking.

"Wait a minute!" Abby's eyes danced. "If Adam *was* spying in the bushes, maybe he saw something that night."

"Like what?" Dunkum asked.

"Maybe he saw the man driving his jeep around Blossom Hill Lane, waiting to steal Honey!"

"I think you might be on to something," said Dunkum.

He hoped so.

★ ★ ★

The Cul-de-sac Kids had another meeting. This time, near a run-down cottage. Shutters were drooping off their hinges. Paint was peeling off the door. Adam Henny's house was a mess.

"Let's find out what Adam knows," Dunkum told the Cul-de-sac Kids. He led his fellow detectives across the street.

Abby carried the ID bracelet. Stacy held Honey's leather collar. The kids lined up on Adam Henny's front steps.

Dunkum poked the doorbell. He hoped they were doing the right thing.

The screen door opened. A woman with white hair peeked through. "May I help you?"

Gulp! Dunkum didn't know what to say. Was this the right house?

Abby stepped up to the door. "Is Adam home?"

The woman smiled. "Oh, he's down the street."

Abby held up the ID bracelet. "Does this belong to Adam?"

The woman nodded. "He's been looking everywhere for it."

Eric spoke up. "Tell him Dunkum Mifflin found it Friday night—in the bushes on our street."

The woman raised her eyebrows. "Friday night, you say?"

"That's right," Dunkum replied. *She must be Adam's grandma*, he thought.

"Well, now, let me think." The woman frowned for a moment. "Adam said he went to a party after the school play. A special party."

"Special?" Abby asked. She looked at Dunkum and the others. There was a question mark in her eyes.

"Oh, yes, and Adam was so pleased," the woman said. "He told me his friends had the party just for him." The wrinkled corners of her mouth curved up. "Is it possible that you are those friends?"

"Uh, no, not really," Dunkum said quickly.

The woman's smile faded. She looked down at the ID bracelet in her hand. "Thanks for returning this. I'll see that Adam gets it."

"Where *is* Adam exactly?" Dunkum asked.

"Just two streets down," she said. "Maybe you can catch him. He's playing detective today, his favorite game."

The kids said good-bye and walked down the steps.

"Sounds like Adam's super lonely," Abby said.

"He'd have to be to make up a story like that," Stacy whispered.

Dunkum heard what Abby and Stacy said. *Having pretend friends can't be any fun*, he thought.

"Any kid who lies about going to a party must be desperate!" Abby said.

"No kidding," Eric said.

Shawn and Jimmy were nodding their heads.

Carly and Dee Dee looked very sad.

Jason did not dance or jive. He stood

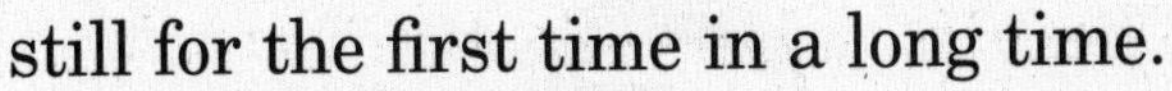

still for the first time in a long time.

Suddenly, Dunkum wished he could change things for Adam. And he knew just what he must do!

TEN

The Cul-de-sac Kids ran down two streets and turned the corner. "Look for Adam's bike," Dunkum said. "It's a faded green one with lots of rust."

They didn't have to look too long. The old bike was propped up against a police car. Three houses down.

Abby gasped. "What are the police doing here?"

"Let's find out." Dunkum led the way to the house.

Adam was sitting on the front step. His

face was smeared with dirt. "Hi, Dunkum. What are *you* doing here?" asked Adam.

"Your grandmother sent us," Dunkum said.

Adam's eyes widened. "She did?"

"She said you were playing detective," Jason said.

Adam's face lit up as two policemen brought a bald man outside. The man was handcuffed.

"Wow! My theory was right," Abby said.

The policemen led the man to the patrol car. They put him in the backseat and zoomed off.

Dunkum stared at Adam. He hardly noticed the boy's crummy old clothes. "Looks like you're an excellent detective."

Adam beamed a smile. "Thanks." He told how he'd tracked down the bad bald guy. "It all started last Friday night. I was spying on your party. After everyone left,

Honey wandered outside. The front door was wide open."

"My fault," Dunkum muttered.

"I sat on the curb just petting her," Adam said.

"And then what happened?" Dunkum asked.

Adam sighed. "I saw a black jeep at the end of the street. It was real late, so I said good-bye to Honey and went home. I didn't even suspect the bald guy of stealing Honey. Not till yesterday."

Abby asked, "What made you curious about him?"

"You told me about your ad, remember?" Adam replied.

Dunkum felt a lump in his throat. Things were finally starting to make sense.

"How'd you ever find this house?" Eric asked.

"I called 9-1-1 and told the police what I'd seen."

"So . . . where's Honey now?" Dunkum asked.

"In the backyard, waiting to go home." Adam got up and went around the side of the house. He returned with Honey.

The Cul-de-sac Kids cheered and rushed to her. Honey's gentle eyes seemed to say, *I'm glad you found me*.

Dunkum thanked Adam for his detective work. "Ellen always believed Honey would be safe," he said. "She missed her dog, but she never worried."

"I should've told you right away what I saw," Adam admitted. "Please tell Ellen I'm sorry I waited."

"Why don't you tell her yourself?" Dunkum said.

"Really?" Adam's face burst into a giant grin. "Do you mean it?"

"Lickety-split!" Dunkum said to Honey.

And she ran between him and Adam all the way back to Blossom Hill Lane.

Abby and the others dashed close behind. They arrived at Dunkum's house, out of breath.

Dunkum told Adam about Honey's ice-cream trick.

Adam's eyes lit up. "Honey does tricks?"

Dunkum nodded and called to Ellen. "Guess who's hungry for a vanilla cone!"

Ellen squealed with delight from her room. "Oh, come here, girl!"

Honey raced upstairs, tail wagging.

"Don't forget about the reward money," Abby said.

But Adam shook his head. "I didn't do this for the money." He looked straight at Dunkum. "But I *do* want something."

Dunkum was sure what Adam wanted. The boy who needed a bath also needed a friend.

Hurrying inside to the kitchen, Dunkum opened the freezer. He reached for a box of ice cream. "It's time to throw a party for a fellow detective." He smiled at Adam Henny.

And Adam smiled back.

About the Author

Beverly Lewis loves to write pets into her stories. In this book, Dunkum's blind cousin has a golden Labrador guide dog. Janet Huntington, who draws the inside pictures, suggested the dog for the story. "Labs are wonderful," says Beverly. "They are gentle and kid-friendly."

Beverly will miss creating The Cul-de-sac Kids books. Every minute she spent writing was much more fun than work. Abby, Shawn, Jason, Stacy, and Dunkum—and all the others—will live in Beverly's heart, and on Blossom Hill Lane, for a very, very long time.

Learn more about Beverly and her books at *www.BeverlyLewis.com*

The Cul-de-Sac Kids Series

Don't miss all the books
in this exciting series
for both boys and girls!

Also by Beverly Lewis

GIRLS ONLY (GO!)
Youth Fiction

Dreams on Ice — *Reach for the Stars*
Only the Best — *Follow the Dream*
A Perfect Match — *Better Than Best*
Photo Perfect

SUMMERHILL SECRETS
Youth Fiction

Whispers Down the Lane — *House of Secrets*
Secret in the Willows — *Echoes in the Wind*
Catch a Falling Star — *Hide Behind the Moon*
Night of the Fireflies — *Windows on the Hill*
A Cry in the Dark — *Shadows Beyond the Gate*

THE HERITAGE OF LANCASTER COUNTY
Adult Fiction

The Shunning — *The Confession*
The Reckoning

OTHER ADULT FICTION
The Postcard
The Crossroad

The Redemption of Sarah Cain

*Sanctuary**

The Sunroom

*with David Lewis

01B

Series for Young Readers*
From Bethany House Publishers

THE ADVENTURES OF CALLIE ANN
by Shannon Mason Leppard
Readers will giggle their way through the true-to-life escapades of Callie Ann Davies and her many North Carolina friends.

ASTROKIDS™
by Robert Elmer
Space scooters? Floating robots? Jupiter ice cream? Blast into the future for out-of-this-world, zero-gravity fun with the AstroKids on space station *CLEO-7*.

BACKPACK MYSTERIES
by Mary Carpenter Reid
This excitement-filled mystery series follows the mishaps and adventures of Steff and Paulie Larson as they strive to help often-eccentric relatives crack their toughest cases.

THE CUL-DE-SAC KIDS
by Beverly Lewis
Each story in this lighthearted series features the hilarious antics and predicaments of nine endearing boys and girls who live on Blossom Hill Lane.

JANETTE OKE'S ANIMAL FRIENDS
by Janette Oke
Endearing creatures from the farm, forest, and zoo discover their place in God's world through various struggles, mishaps, and adventures.

THREE COUSINS DETECTIVE CLUB®
by Elspeth Campbell Murphy
Famous detective cousins Timothy, Titus, and Sarah-Jane learn compelling Scripture-based truths while finding—and solving—intriguing mysteries.

*(ages 7-10)